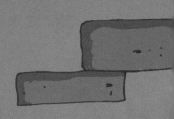

PEUK 2326

Published by Ladybird Books Ltd
A Penguin Company
Penguin Books Ltd, 80 Strand, London, WC2R ORL, England
Penguin Books Australia Ltd, Camberwell, Victoria, Australia
Penguin Group (NZ), cnr Airborne and Rosedale Roads,
Albany, Auckland 1310, New Zealand
All rights reserved

ISBN-13: 978-1-84422-641-2
ISBN-10: 1-8442-2641-7

4 6 8 10 9 7 5 3

Ladybird and the device of a ladybird are trademarks
of Ladybird Books Ltd

Printed in Italy

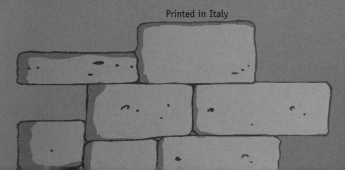

SCOOBY-DOO!™

the
Snack
Catcher

Shaggy, Scooby and the gang
were at the Coolsville Bake-Off
Contest.
"Like get a noseful of that!"
said Shaggy as he and Scooby
sniffed the air.
"Rmmm-rmmm!"

6

Scooby and Shaggy had entered the contest.
They were going to bake Scooby Snacks.
"Like, this is the best!" Shaggy smiled.
"And the winner gets free pizza for a year!"

Velma, Fred and Daphne grabbed the supplies.
"These bags weigh a ton!" Velma said.
"What's in here?" asked Daphne.
"Ingredients," said Shaggy. "Flour, sugar… "
Then Scooby pulled out a box.
"Rizza!" Scooby cried.

8

"There's no pizza in Scooby Snacks,"
Velma said.
Shaggy took a big cheesy bite.
"It's not for the snacks," he explained. "It's for
the cooks!"
"Rat's right!" said Scooby.

"Humph!" said skinny Ms Pinchface, in the next booth. "What noisy eating!"

Shaggy and Scooby watched Ms Pinchface wash beans for a veggie pie. Then they spied the Tubb Twins making double fudge brownies.

"Like, let's get cooking!" said Shaggy.

10

Scooby took out more ingredients. Then they pulled out baking sheets, dough cutters, chef hats, aprons, and finally: another pizza! "Whew!" Shaggy yawned. "I'm tired. If I weren't hungry for Scooby Snacks, I would take a nap. Like, let's hurry, Scoob. So we can snooze!"

11

Shaggy grabbed the flour. Whoosh! It spilled on the floor. Scooby grabbed the eggs. Crack! They smashed on the table.

"Pour!" Shaggy shouted. "Knead! Mix!"

Finally the dough was ready.
Shaggy and Scooby shoved the
snacks into the oven. In a flash,
they fell asleep.
Across the room, Velma, Fred
and Daphne heard a scream
and a thud.

It was Ms Pinchface, a bag of beans at her feet.
"What's wrong?" cried Daphne.
"There's a monster!" Ms Pinchface shouted.
"Over by my table! It's all white and spooky-
looking, without any eyes!"

A rumbling noise shook the room. "I see
something on the other side!" Daphne cried.
"Let's go!" said Fred.
Velma, Fred and Daphne ran closer. The
noise grew louder.

But as they reached the cooking booth, the noise had stopped. The monster was gone.

"Like, quiet down, you guys," Shaggy said. "We're sleeping here!"

"We're sorry," said Daphne. "But Ms Pinchface saw a monster!"

"A monster?" Shaggy said. "Wake up, Scooby. There's a monster…"

Bing! The oven timer went off.

"Ronster!" said Scooby, jumping up.

17

"That was the oven," said Velma. Shaggy
opened the oven door carefully.
"Zoinks!" cried Shaggy. "It's empty!"
"No Rooby Racks?" said Scooby.
"The monster ate your snacks!" said Ms Pinchfac

"Look at this!" said Velma. She pointed to handprints on the oven door… yellow ones!
"And rook!" cried Scooby. There were huge paw prints on the floor. Monster prints!
"Let's look for clues!" said Fred.
"Scooby and Shaggy can guard the oven," Velma said.

"Not even for free pizza!" Shaggy said, terrified.

"Would you do it for Scooby Snacks?" Velma asked.

Scooby sniffed hungrily. So did Shaggy. "Rooby Racks? Rokay!"

Velma, Daphne and Fred followed the trail of paw prints.

Shaggy and Scooby were alone. All at once,
they spied a trail of crumbs.
"This could lead to the monster!" said Shaggy.
"Or more Rooby Racks!" said Scooby.
They followed the crumbs.

Scooby licked up one crumb, then another.
"Hey!" said Shaggy. "Leave some for me."
He gobbled some up, too. Slurp, slurp. They
kept their heads to the ground. Bump! They
crashed into Daphne, Fred and Velma.

Shaggy rubbed his head.

"Like, hey! We're back where we started. And so are you!"

"The crumbs circle the oven, and so do the paw prints," said Velma.

She peeked at Scooby's paws. "White!" said Velma. Next she looked at Shaggy's hands. "Yellow!" she cried. Fred wiped crumbs from Shaggy's shirt.

"These are like the ones on the floor!" he said.

"Shaggy, did you eat the Scooby Snacks?"

"Well, maybe I woke up from my nap for a minute, and ate some."

"What about you, Scooby-Doo?" Velma said.

Scooby shrugged. "I rate rome, roo."

"There is no monster!" Velma said. "We saw something white. But it was only Shaggy and Scooby in an apron and hat! Shaggy's hands are yellow from the egg yolk. He made the handprints! And Scooby's paws are white from flour. He made the paw prints! You both ate the snacks. And you didn't even know it!"

"Oh no! That means we are out of the contest," said Shaggy.

"Now you can try all the other food!" said Velma. Shaggy took a bite of the veggie pie. "Like, this is delicious!" He eyed all the tables. "And we've only just begun!" Scooby grinned. "Scooby-Dooby-Doo!"